The Silver Fox and the Great Hunter

Willie J. Boyd's

T H E

The Silver Fox and the Great Hunter

Edited by
Margaret Ford-Taylor
and Janie M. Boyd
Cover Design by
Frederick Burton

Copyright © 2020 by Willie James Boyd

Written and published by: Willie J. Boyd
Edited by: Margaret Ford Taylor and Janie M. Boyd
Cover design by: Frederick L. Burton

ISBN 978-0-9971222-1-3

Printed in the United States of America

In Memoriam

To my father
George Washington Boyd

~

My mother
Jennie Florence Boyd

~

My older sister
Ceteria Ann Saahir

~

My little sister
Geneva (Gen-Gen) Boyd

Acknowledgements

All glory to God, from whom all blessings are possible!

Thanks to my beautiful and talented wife, Janie.

Special thanks to my mentor and dear friend MFT (Margaret Ford Taylor)!

A very special thank you to my friend and buddy, graphic artist, Frederick Burton, for his encouragement and yeomen's work, and who reminds me, "it's all about the journey!"

Willie J. Boyd

About the Contributors

Willie J. Boyd is the creator of The Be Good Kids© and the force behind The Be Good Kids© 5-day Greeting Card System; The Be Good Kids© Curriculum (For Pre-Schoolers and Kindergartners - A Character-Building Project); and the first book, "The Be Good Kids© What A Bully Really Looks Like." Mr. Boyd has worked in stage, television, and print for over 25 years.

Margaret Ford-Taylor "MFT" is a twice Emmy-nominated actor and writer. Her first Emmy nomination was for her performance in the public television production of "American Women: Echoes and Dreams." Author of more than 40 critically acknowledged and nationally-produced stage works, MFT's second Emmy nomination was as writer of the ABC television documentary, "The Second Reconstruction," narrated by Ossie Davis.

Janie M. Boyd has a B.B.A. from Howard University, with a major in marketing. She is a Lifetime Certified Purchasing Manager, having recently retired from the Technology Portfolio of the U.S. Postal Service, with a concentration on Supplier Market Analysis and Research.

Frederick Burton is the book designer and graphic artist for The Be Good Kids© greeting card system. After graduating from Cooper School of Art, he enjoyed a successful career in advertising and design for a major retailer and the United States Postal Service, where he received local and national awards. Today he owns and operates Frederick Burton Design LLC in Mentor, Ohio; creating exhibits, outdoor advertising, banners, signs, corporate identity and collateral materials, locally and nationally. He is the author of "Cleveland's Gospel Music" and the founder of the Gospel Music Historical Society, a 501(c)(3) public charity.

Good Thought Productions, LLC
PO Box 1291
Kernersville, NC 27285

www.GoodThoughtProductions.com

Once upon a time long, long, long, ago there lived a King known as The Great Hunter. Now this great King owed his reputation to the fact that during his reign he was reported to have slain every wild animal known to man, and from the earliest of age every child in the kingdom could recite the awe-inspiring tales that had produced the magnificent trophy room that was the King's pride and glory.

Still — even as he enjoyed and relished his fame as The Great Hunter, a nagging doubt grew in the King's mind in proportion to his notoriety. You see, from birth, he had heard stories of an elusive, and possibly, mythical animal called The Silver Fox. He did not know if the tales were true but the more his trophy room expanded and his list of known and slain predators diminished, the more he wondered about the reality of The Silver Fox. In fact, he thought about it year after year, month after month, day and night, night and day until, finally, it became an absolute obsession.

One morning, after a long and sleepless night he summoned his chief advisor.

"I want to know — I have to know — if it is fact or fable," he demanded. "Does the Silver Fox truly exist?" He then issued a proclamation that startled and galvanized the entire kingdom. He offered a golden purse of 5,000 talents to anyone who could prove or disprove the existence of the Silver Fox.

Once initiated, the search stretched on for years as every man, woman and child in the Kingdom involved themselves in the quest to win the golden purse. In addition, the passing years did nothing to abate the King's determination to find the truth regarding the Silver Fox. As a matter of fact, in the course of time his obsession grew to the point that he added to the incentive by, first, doubling and then tripling the award amount.

His persistence finally paid off. A handsome convoy of prize seekers gained an audience with the King and assured him that there was, indeed, such an animal as the Silver Fox. The proof, they reported, was held by an old African Griot who resided in the deepest, darkest and most unexplored country of the Sudan in the Province of Tambura. The Griot knew the exact location of the mysterious land of the Silver Fox.

Elated, the King said to himself in feverish anticipation, "I know what I will do. I will first visit this old Griot and convince him to lead me to this place of mystery. Once there, I will finally lay eyes on this Silver Fox. I will study every move he makes, no matter how long it takes; and when the time is right, I will slay him and bring him home to add him to my collection! Then and only then will my trophy room be complete!"

"But what of our reward," exclaimed the leader of the group, "your promise of three golden purses of 5,000 talents each?!"

"Oh, you will have your reward," replied the King. "In fact, you will travel with me and as soon as I lay eyes on this Silver Fox, you will receive what you will so richly deserve."

But the leader was a shrewd man. "Who will guard the golden purses until we return?" he demanded.
"Oh, the reward will travel with us," said the King. "You will not be denied one minute of your treasure once I have seen the Silver Fox."

This satisfied even the sharpest skeptic; and after hurried, but careful, preparation, the King and his entourage set off excitedly for the land of the Silver Fox. If the search for proof of the mysterious animal had taken a long time, the journey to confront him seemed ten times as long; and even though the King had been on countless hunting expeditions, this trip seemed to take an eternity, so anxious was he to come face to face with this unparalleled foe!

The day finally did come when they reached their destination! Although at first they had seen no one, the increasing volume of drumbeats signaled their approach. When the King and his convoy finally arrived at the village of the Griot, the natives came from everywhere to see this strange group that was totally unlike anything they had ever seen or imagined. As if of one mind, all eyes sought out and lit up with impressed amazement at the sight of the regally imposing figure of the leader, the King, who stalked with unabashed superiority and to the accompaniment of the increasing sounds of the drum beat, up the path to where he had been directed the Griot awaited him.

Upon reaching his destination, the King suddenly stopped, throwing his head back and squaring his shoulders in one commanding movement as he took an imposing stance in front of a figure that was in the center of a group of waiting natives. The crowd that had followed the King and his subjects immediately closed in behind them as the drumming sounds came to a crashing halt!

At the silence, the King found himself standing in front of the Griot, a very old man with a very long white beard and eyes that shone like gold.

He was dressed in a white loosely draped loin cloth which, even seated, accentuated a long, statuesque neck and body. As the Griot slowly stretched upward to a standing position to greet the King, he appeared to grow stopping only when he was a full head taller than the monarch. For an infinity the two men stared into each other's eyes, the King looking up, the Griot looking down. Slowly, the Griot raised his right arm indicating the path from which the King and his followers had just come. The King turned in the direction indicated by the Griot, observing the arrival of a figure which he knew could only be the village witch doctor, the Jolly Bar, who he had learned of during his long journey to this place. The crowd that had parted for the arrival of the Jolly Bar moved solidly back into place as the witch doctor took a stance a few feet from the King. Silently, the Griot melted back to his sitting position and sat, immobile, eyes intently focused on the group in the space before him.

It was midday, sunny and brilliantly bright and there was no sound. The Jolly Bar stood motionless, ignoring the King while staring up into the heavens as if waiting for a sign. The crowd appeared not to breathe. The silence was deafening. Suddenly, with a click, a star appeared as if it was night, a phenomenon which seemed to release the Jolly Bar from his spell and be began dancing slowly around and around the

King, finally separating him from the rest of his group. As the space between the King and his followers widened, the movement of the Jolly Bar grew faster and faster and faster! Around and around the King he spun, his speed becoming so intense that the body in the multicolored costuming blurred to the image of a whirling, twirling spinning top! Time passed until, suddenly, the Jolly Bar stopped in front of the King as if on a dime, his face almost touching the Great Hunter's.

The King appeared to remain undaunted and unimpressed while the rest of his party stood frozen in mesmerized shock, one member actually collapsing to his knees in trembling amazement. Tension mounted as the Great Hunter's eyes locked with those of the witch doctor, each communicating his thoughts without words:

"Are you sure?" asked the Jolly Bar finally.

"Yes." replied the Great Hunter.

"Then let the ceremony begin!" called out the Witch Doctor and with that, the natives began encircling the Great Hunter. As if by silent command, the sound of drums began once again.

Ta-boom! Ta-boom! Ta-boom! Ta-boom!

Immediately, the natives began stomping their feet to what turned out to be the rhythm of the Great Hunter's heart beat! The Jolly Bar shook his rattle and began to chant.

"As you stand there blessed
with the power to see clear do not be confused
because what your eyes see is backwards...
Wanting to tell everyone who does not understand
why you, as a Great Hunter, are being taught
to live only to die
without knowing the reason why.
Yet you feel you must tell them why,
but don't
because they can't hear you.
Understanding that it
is backwards before me in the word time,
you are being forced into silence
until you can say it backwards right.
Well, the vision should be coming clear
and silence is the way to hear
and to conquer the fear over those
who are dear,
your action is the only thing they will hear.
In life you do it all, from A to Z;
you dot the I and you cross the T;
then you view life backwards.
You turn your eyes inward to view
the true you,

and the world will see your beauty too.

The drumming stopped as abruptly as it had begun. The Griot rose and entered the circle. Commandingly, he said to the King,

"The words you have just heard are engraved here upon this scroll. Remember the words. Do not forget them."

He then handed the scroll to the Jolly Bar who moved to the circle where he went from native to native, stopping for each one to step forward, place his hand on the scroll and repeat, "Remember the words. Do not forget them. Remember the words. Do not forget them." The ritual seemed to take a lifetime but not once did the King flinch or otherwise show any sign of fatigue or discomfort. When the last native had stepped back into line, the Jolly Bar took the scroll and returned it to the Griot.

By this time, the scroll was luminous and glowing! Extending the scroll to the King, the Griot said in a resounding voice,

"Keep the scroll with you at all times and it will remind you to always be yourself!"

The Great Hunter reached out to receive the scroll and as he touched it, for seconds, the world stopped. Out of that eternity the Jolly Bar spoke to the Griot.

"He is now ready to use his ears as his eyes," he whispered. The Griot nodded.

"Listen closely," the Griot finally said to the Great Hunter. "You are almost ready for the journey you seek, but first I must speak of times when there were not men in the world; when animals, plants and the air were pure and, finally, when your ears see what your heart desires, you will begin to fade into that world but you must still remember to guard who you are."

The Griot sat crossed legged and everyone followed suit. Time moved unnoticed as he spoke of many many things and told of many animals and their special gifts bestowed upon them by their Creator. The Griot spoke of Pegasus, the winged horse whose wings were made lighter than the lightest cloud. He spoke of the Phoenix, whose gift was the ability to rise from the fire of his own ashes in rebirth.

After an immeasurable time, the Griot said,

"Of all the canine that ever existed, the rarest of them all is the Silver Fox."

At these words, the Great Hunter and his entire entourage, many of whom had slumped into abject fatigue, became alert. Finally, many of them thought, they were going to come to the end of this torturous journey. Finally, they were about to be rewarded for all of their pain and suffering during this miserable pilgrimage. Finally, they had come to the end! Without exception every eye was now concentrated on the old Griot. The Great Hunter's heart began to race in anticipation of his conquest to come.

What no one in the King's party took note of was the second the Griot had uttered the word "fox" the Great Hunter had begun to fade.

In the meantime, the Griot continued to talk in a slow measured undertone.

"Now, just as certain other animals received special gifts, so did the Silver Fox. His unique gift was and continues to be that in the hour glass of life, he exists 15 minutes in time before all other living creatures. The Silver Fox was so grateful for what he had received that he made a vow that he would never allow himself to be so dazzled by any other animal's gift or abilities that he forgot to appreciate his own special gift.

His vow was that he would make the most of what had been given to him. And because the Silver Fox always kept this vow, he never left himself and because he never left himself, from the beginning of time he was able to avoid capture by anything or anybody.

The Griot had continued to talk but the King had ceased listening long ago. His mind raced ahead formulating plans to capture the Silver Fox.

"All I wanted to know was if the Silver Fox truly exists," thought the King, his heart thumping. "Now that I know that he does, he does not stand a chance against me, The Great Hunter." So deep in thought was he, he lost all sense of time. The words the Griot had spoken, faded from his mind. The only sound he continued to hear was the pounding of his own heartbeat.

"I will learn everything there is to learn about this so-called Silver Fox. I will walk like him. I will talk like him. I will think like him. I will be like him in every way. He will not escape me and when the time is right, he shall belong to me."

"The Silver Fox has many, many characteristics that he was able to obtain only in being himself," the Griot concluded. He paused a moment, then finally stood as did the entire assemblage. He walked three steps closer to the fading, yet regal image of the King and said, "Close your eyes."

The King did as he was told. The Griot continued, "From now on you may rely on your hearing to guide you and remember the writing on the scroll. It will also aid you in your return to your own reality. Now go!"

The Great Hunter felt himself being swept away as if floating on a warm dry breeze.

The men who had traveled with him began to panic when it became clear that the Great Hunter had disappeared. In his place there was a small residue of a cloud-like substance. They also realized they were surrounded by natives who pressed in closer to where they stood. Without another word the Griot turned and began to walk away. The Jolly Bar spoke to the group.

"Have no fear. No one will harm you here. You will simply remain here and serve until your leader returns."

"But what of our gold?" one man complained. "We were promised three bags each."

"I know nothing of what you speak," said the Jolly Bar. You may keep with you whatever you have brought to this place. We have no need of it. Yet you will still serve until your leader returns. He was given instructions and your ultimate fate is up to him."

With that the Jolly Bar turned and strode away as the natives closed in around the group and all began to move as if with a tide in the opposite direction.

In the meantime, the Great Hunter stood transfixed by the brightness of his surroundings.

"So this is the domain of the Silver Fox," he exclaimed to himself. Why, it appears to be right in the middle of a rainbow!"

At the same time, he became aware of a bright, cheerful sound the likes of which he had never heard before! Someone was singing! Moving as if in a trance he began climbing to the top of a multicolored hill which had suddenly appeared before him.

As he reached the crest, the King beheld the most amazing sight he had ever seen! It was The Silver Fox! The glorious, magnificent creature that has avoided capture since the beginning of time! There he was! Bathed in a shower of multicolored light and glowingly revealed! Singing and twirling, dancing and prancing and emanating the sweetest of sounds! The Silver Fox!

"A ripidee doo dot didot diday!
It's the best way to feel!
And if I could share with the world the way I truly feel
now,
I'd spread it all around!
A ripidee doo dot didot diday!
I'm proud to be that what I am
And if you want to know, to know the secret way
you have to listen to what I say. Hey!
A ripidee doo dot didot diday!
It's the best way to feel!
And if you want to know, to know the real deal,
be quiet and real still:
Think positive, and you'll be positive
and everything will come to you.
But you must know what to do, to do do,
you must know what to do.
A ripidee doo dot didot diday!
It's the best way to feel!
And if you want to know, to know the secret way
you have to listen to what I say:
For all the thoughts coming to you,
you must pay attention
and pick out the best ones due to you.
Erase the bad thoughts and they'll go away
and you'll have time to play. Hey!
A ripidee doo dot didot diday!
It's the best way to feel!

Do what I tell you and you can always play...
and do it your own special way!

The Great Hunter had regained enough of his arrogance to scoff at the last words sang by the Silver Fox.

"Your own special way?!" he scornfully thought. "Well, we'll see about that! I don't know why that shaft of light seems to follow your every footstep; but I have some nice candle light that you'll look perfect under in my trophy room. Even though you walk upright like a man and your fur is the brightest and the most precious in the land, you'll still be part of my overall plan!"

Even as the King thought, the Silver Fox pranced out of his view and over the next hill. The Great Hunter literally shook himself free of all the mesmerizing sensations caused by the splendid sight of the Silver Fox. Briefly, he glanced around for his entourage. Their absence did not deter him. "Nothing, nothing will stand in the way of me completing this mission," he thought.

"I will complete the task without them and prove for all time who the greatest hunter of all ages really is, the Silver Fox has been able to avoid capture because he knew more about his would be captors than they knew about him. I will not make the same mistake."

With that, he proceeded to do exactly what he had promised to do when he began the expedition.

First, he followed the Silver Fox all over the beautiful rainbow watching his every move. Each time he got a certain distance from him the Silver Fox would prance away. The Great Hunter had stalked countless other animals before; but none gave him more joy than this one. He did everything the Silver Fox did. He walked like him. He talked like him. He ate like him. He slept like him. He even tried to think like him. Finally realizing the impossibility of this he said, "Never mind. I don't need to think like him. The rest is enough." So he practiced and practiced and practiced being like the Silver Fox. He followed him night and day. He was enjoying himself so much he did not realize he had misplaced the scroll; and when he finally did notice, he did not care having convinced himself that it was unnecessary to his mission.

The day finally came when the Great Hunter knew his time had come. He had watched the Silver Fox all that day. He was certain the beautiful animal had forgotten all about him so busy was he prancing and dancing and singing. He had tarried in this particular meadow much longer than was his habit "And that", thought the Great Hunter, "will be his undoing."

The King stealthily approached the meadow stopping just behind a clump of trees located a short distance from where the Silver Fox was basking in the sun and enjoying his play with unusual abandon. The King noted that instead of moving away as he approached, the Silver Fox seemed to increase his pleasure of the moment.

"Enjoy, my friend," whispered the Great Hunter dropping to one knee. "This is your last frolic with the sun."

With that, he pointed his musket directly at the heart of the Silver Fox, expertly raising his finger to the trigger. At the same time, he caught sight of his hand, which had ceased to be a hand at all. It was a paw! He took inventory of his stature and, behold, he was a fox himself!

"Ah, I'm a fox! How can this be?!" He lowered his musket in dismay, dropped to his knees, and mumbled barely audibly, "I'm not going to shoot a fellow fox! A fox like that I am surely!"

The Great Hunter, the King, had forgotten who he was. And with that, he began to fade again. As the King dissolved slowly into history, the Silver Fox revealed his gift to him:

"Because of my special gift, I have always known every move you were planning to make 15 minutes before you did it.

I also know you have become what you have become because despite warnings, you did not appreciate your own special gifts from the Creator but sought, instead, to leave yourself and duplicate me for your own nefarious purpose. Now you have no gift!"

Finally the King was blown away by a harsh wind. Only the memory was left behind.

It is rumored that a new kingdom arose not long after the disappearance of the Great Hunter. The realm had a remarkable monarch who moved in delightful measures and founded The King's Sanctuary for all animals to be able to live in abundance throughout their lives.

I'll not say it … Oh maybe I will. Poetic justice!

The moral of this story is: Always be yourself!

THE END

Book Club Notes

www.ingramcontent.com/pod-product-compliance
Lightning Source LLC
Chambersburg PA
CBHW071229130626
46555CB00004B/1913